Little Blue Car

Gwen Grant

Illustrated by Susan Hellard

ORCHARD BOOKS

For my granddaughter Laura Anne Grant
G.G.

ORCHARD BOOKS
338 Euston Road,
London NW1 3BH
Orchard Books Australia
Hachette Children's Books
Level 17/207 Kent Street, Sydney, NSW 2000

First published in Great Britain in 1991
This paperback edition published 2006

Text © Gwen Grant 1991
Illustrations © Susan Hellard 1991

ISBN 1 84616 279 3

1 3 5 7 9 10 8 6 4 2

Printed in China

Once upon a time, there was a factory that made cars. Red cars, yellow cars, black cars and green cars pink cars and one little blue car.

When the little blue car was made, he was put outside to sit in the sunshine.

"I am so warm," sighed the little blue car. "I do wish I could go to the seaside."

He looked at the gate. Through the gate he could see a road. "I'm going," he said.

And the little blue car ran down the road to the sea.

When he got to the seaside, he ran on to the sand and into the sea without stopping.

The waves tickled his tyres. Fish swam and jumped all round him.
"Who are you?" the fish asked.
"I am little blue car," he said.

The little blue car stayed in the sea all day. He didn't notice it was getting dark. Then it started to get cold and his tyres were frozen.

"Brrrrr!" he shivered. "I think I'll come out now."

When he got on to the sand, he saw that everyone had gone.

"I don't like the seaside any more!" he cried. "I want to go home."

The little blue car drove away and left the seaside far behind.

"It's very dark," he whispered. "I can't see where I'm going." Then he stopped. He was too scared to go any further.

Over the hill came a big shiny bus
with all its lights on.

"What are you doing here?" asked the
bus.

"I'm lost," said the little blue car.
He was very unhappy.
"Why don't you put your lights on
and then you'll know where you are?"
the bus said.
"Have I got lights?"
"Of course you've got lights. Press
that switch there."
The little blue car pressed the switch,
and on came all his lights.

"Goodbye," said the bus as he
trundled away.
The little blue car wasn't frightened
any more. He had his lights on.

Now, he was tired.
"Ohhhhh," he yawned, and his
bonnet opened as wide as it could go.

Then he saw a sign. LAYBY, the
sign said.
The little blue car pulled off the road
into the dark quiet layby.

There were trees in the layby. There
were owls and foxes with shining eyes.
"Who are you?" the owls asked.
But the little blue car was fast asleep.

When he woke up in the morning, he was frozen stiff. His whole body was white with frost.

"Oh!" he cried. "I'm freezing."

"I don't like this layby any more," the little blue car wailed. "I want to go home."

Down the road came an enormous
lorry. The lorry stopped when it saw the
little blue car.

"BLAAAAARE. BLAAAAAARE,"
hooted the lorry. "You look very cold."

"I am cold," the little blue car said.
"Well, why don't you switch your
heater on and get warm?" the lorry
asked.

"Have I got a heater?"
"Of course you've got
a heater. Press that switch
there."

The little blue car
pressed the switch.
On came the heater.
The heater made
him warm.

"Goodbye," the lorry
hooted, and roared away.
The little blue car wasn't
frightened any more.
He had his lights on.
He had his heater on.

He drove down the wide road. He was tired of moving. He wanted to play. Then he saw a field and the little blue car ran straight on to the grass.

The grass tickled his tyres. Lambs played and jumped all round him. They looked through his windows.

"Who are you?" the lambs asked.

"I am little blue car," he said.

The little blue car played in the field all morning. He didn't notice the sun had gone. Then he heard a noise on his roof.

Pitter patter pitter patter pitter patter pit.

"Whatever's that?" he said.

He drove across the field. Then he stopped. He couldn't see through the water on his windscreen.

"I don't like this field any more," the little blue car cried. "I want to go home."

Over the field came a bright red tractor with all its lights on.

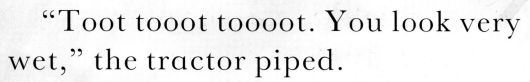

"Toot tooot toooot. You look very wet," the tractor piped.

" I am wet," said the little blue car. "And I can't see a thing."

"Why don't you put your windscreen wipers on, so that you can see where you're going?" the tractor asked.

"Have I got windscreen wipers?"
"Of course you've got windscreen wipers. Press that switch there."
The little blue car pressed the switch and on came his windscreen wipers. Swish swish. Swish swish.

"Goodbye goodbye," The tractor rumbled away.

The little blue car wasn't frightened any more. He had his lights on. He had his heater on. He had his windscreen wipers on.

The little blue car drove out of the field. The rain stopped and the sun began to shine.

He drove straight down the road, all the way back to the factory.
He drove straight in through the factory gates.

He could see all the other cars. Best of all, he could see his very own parking space.

"Hooray," said the little blue car. "At last. I'm home."